D0480142

**For Amy**

**OXFORD**
UNIVERSITY PRESS

Great Clarendon Street, Oxford OX2 6DP

Oxford is a registered trade mark of Oxford University Press
in the UK and in certain other countries

Text and Illustrations © An Vrombaut 2003
The moral rights of the author/illustrator have been asserted

First published in 2003

All rights reserved.
British Library Cataloguing in Publication Data available

ISBN 0-19-279092-7 HB
ISBN 0-19-272547-5 PB

3 5 7 9 10 8 6 4 2

Typeset in Kristen/Siesta/Fiesta
Printed and bound in China

# Smile, Crocodile, Smile

# An Vrombaut

OXFORD

UNIVERSITY PRESS

It's time to wake up
at the Mango Tree House.

Ruby brushes her rabbit teeth.

Liam brushes his leopard teeth.

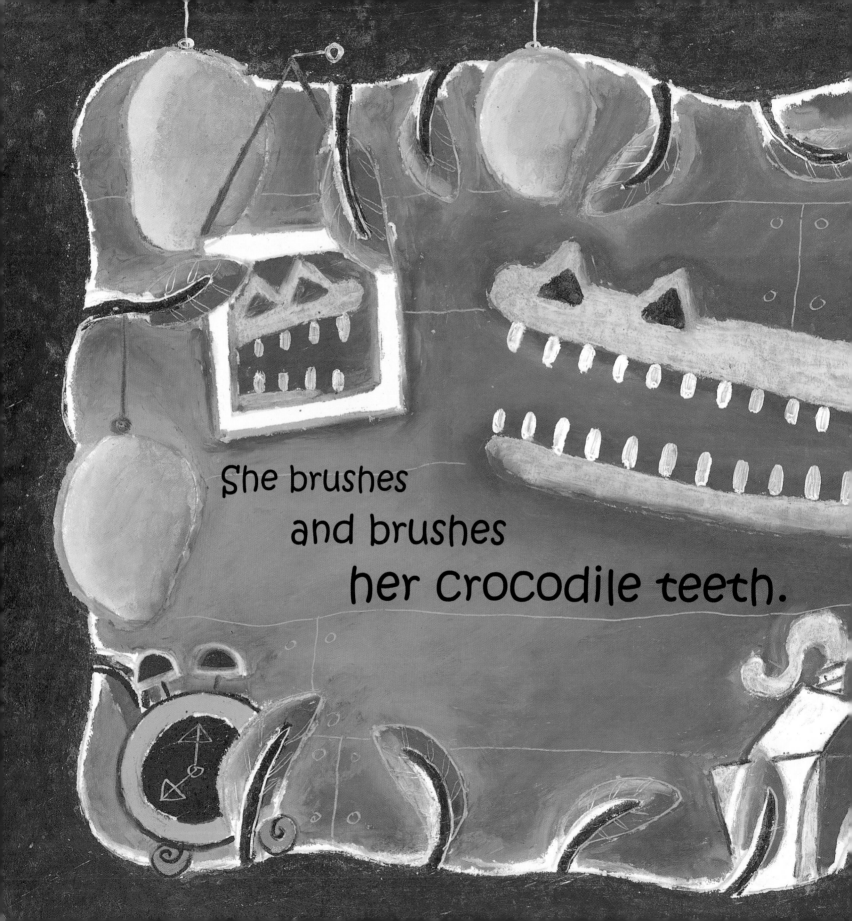

She brushes
and brushes
her crocodile teeth.

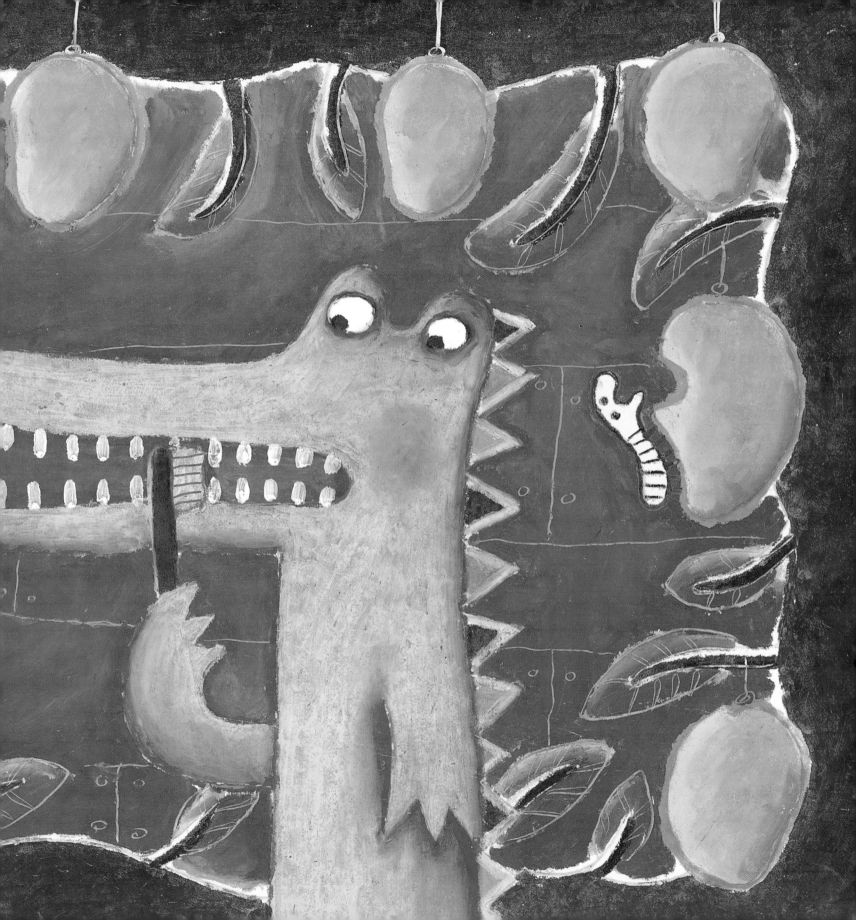

It's playtime
at the Mango Tree House.

Ruby builds a sandcastle.

Liam races on
his scooter.

Max makes a mess.

Zoë plays with a puzzle.

And Clarabella?

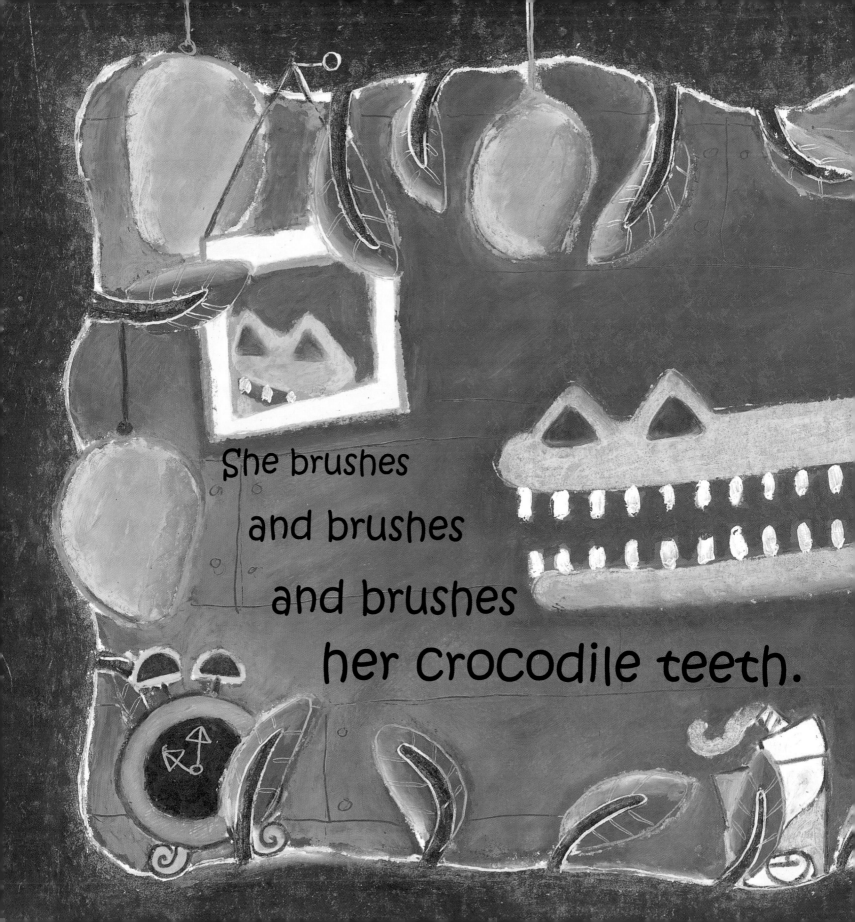

She brushes
and brushes
and brushes
her crocodile teeth.

It's lunchtime
at the Mango Tree House.

Ruby nibbles a yummy mango.

Liam licks a mango lolly.

Max sips a mango milkshake.

Zoë munches a
mango sandwich.

And Clarabella?

She brushes
and brushes
and brushes
and brushes
her crocodile teeth.

It's tumble time
at the Mango Tree House.

Ruby does a roly-poly.

Liam makes a leopard leap.

Max bounces up and down.

Zoë spins round and round and round and round.

And Clarabella?

She has brushed ALL
her crocodile teeth
and is ready
to play!

But where are her friends?

It's almost bedtime
at the Mango Tree House . . .

'We've come to brush
our teeth,' say Zoë
and Liam
and Max
and Ruby.

# And Clarabella?

She sighs a
L  O  N  G
crocodile
sigh . . .

Then Ruby has an idea.

'It's surprise time
at the Mango Tree House!'

A crocodile toothbrush for Clarabella!

'Hurray!' cheer Ruby and Liam
and Max and Zoë.
'Tomorrow we can all play
together.'

And Clarabella?

She smiles a **BIG** crocodile smile!